For Ilaria, Alessia and Rob
D.M.

First published in 2022 by Nosy Crow Ltd

The Crow's Nest, 14 Baden Place, Crosby Row, London, SE1 1YW

Nosy Crow Eireann Ltd, 44 Orchard Grove, Kenmare, Co Kerry, V93 FY22, Ireland

www.nosycrow.com

ISBN 978 1 83994 496 3 (HB)

ISBN 978 1 83994 497 0 (PB)

Nosy Crow and associated logos are trademarks
and/or registered trademarks of Nosy Crow Ltd.

A CIP catalogue record for this book is available from the British Library.

Printed in China

Papers used by Nosy Crow are made from wood grown in sustainable forests.

10 9 8 7 6 5 4 3 2 1 (HB)

10 9 8 7 6 5 4 3 2 1 (PB)

# Ruffles

and the **cosy, cosy bed**

David Melling

This is **Ruffles.**

Ruffles **loves** . . .

singing . . .

scratching . . .

eating . . .

fetching . . .

sniffing . . .

chewing . . .

digging . . .

running . . .

and sleeping.

Not the towel . . .

not the box . . .

not the cupboard . . .

not the racket . . .

not the laundry basket . . .

not the mat . . .

not the chair . . .

not the bucket . . .

and not the colander!

Ruffles needs somewhere quiet,
cosy and safe. Where can he go?

Suddenly, Ruffles has an idea . . .

. . . and he runs back to his very own bed.

It's quiet. It's cosy. It's safe.
It's the best place to be.

In his very . . .

own . . .

bed . . .

he has his very . . .

own . . .

cushion . . .

and his very . . .

own . . .

blankie.

Now the loud night noises
don't seem so bad.

And before long, the thunderstorm has gone!

Ruffles loves . . .

singing . . .

scratching . . .

eating . . .

fetching . . .

sniffing . . .

chewing . . .

digging . . .

running . . .

and sleeping.

But most of all, Ruffles **loves** his very own bed.
It's the best place to be . . .

until morning!